DUNCAN CARRIES A KING

A DONKEY'S TALE

Written by Dan Taylor & Damon J. Taylor
Illustrated by Damon J. Taylor

Duncan the donkey was useless. At least, that's what he thought. You see, all of his friends were finding that God had created them for certain jobs. But Duncan didn't have a job to do.

His friend Carrie the camel carried water to thirsty workers from the well in town.

And Omar the ox turned the grindstone that ground the grain into flour for bread.

Duncan thought that maybe he was just too young to have a job. But Horace the horse was the same age as Duncan, and he was already carrying a soldier on his back.

I REMEMBER WHEN WE USED TO PLAY IN THE PEN. NOW LOOK AT HIM!

When Duncan asked if he could try carrying a soldier, Horace replied, "You need to practice a long time if you ever want to carry someone as special as a soldier."

Duncan wanted to have a job. He wanted God to use him in some way.

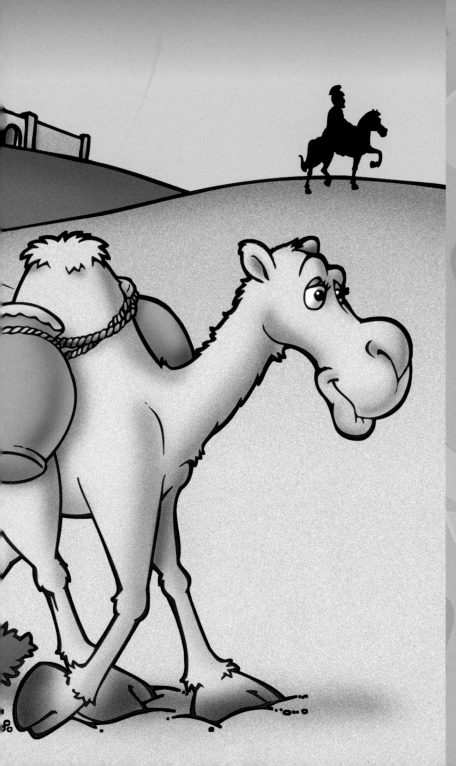

"I wish I knew what I could do!" he brayed. But Duncan wasn't big, like Horace, or strong, like Omar. He couldn't work all day without getting thirsty, as Carrie could. "I'm useless," he said sadly.

One day, some of Jesus' friends came to Duncan's village. They were looking for someone to do a very special job. Jesus had sent them to find a donkey that no one had ever ridden before.

"The donkey that I want is in a village just outside of Jerusalem," He had told them. "Please go get him and bring him to me. If anyone asks you, 'Why are you taking that donkey?' just tell them, 'The Lord needs it.' They will let you take him."

Jesus said this because of something that God, His Father, had promised—through the words of the prophet Zechariah—more than five hundred years earlier. He said that when His Son came into the world, He would ride into Jerusalem on a donkey.

See, your king comes to you, righteous and having salvation, gentle and riding on a donkey, on a colt, the foal of a donkey.

Zechariah 9:9

When Jesus' friends saw Duncan, they knew he was the donkey Jesus had told them to find.

As they tied a rope around Duncan's neck, the soldier riding Horace stopped them. "Here, take my horse instead," he offered. "He's much stronger and better for the task."

"He's right," thought Duncan, "Horace would do a better job than I can. I'm just a donkey."

"I have no training. I'm not fast, I'm not strong, and I'm not as handsome as Horace."

That's when Duncan heard from God. . . .

"Duncan, I have a special job and I want *you* to do it. My Son, Jesus, is going to enter Jerusalem today on the back of a donkey that has never been ridden, just like the prophet Zechariah said. I have chosen you, Duncan, to be that donkey."

Duncan smiled a big smile as Jesus' friends told the soldier, "No, Jesus only wants *this* donkey." He finally had a job!

"Ah, my friends. You have done a fine job," Jesus said. "This is exactly the donkey I wanted."

Duncan looked into Jesus' eyes and his feelings of uselessness slipped away. Duncan knew he was being used by God and God's Son, and that made him very happy.

And with that, Jesus rode on Duncan's back into the city of Jerusalem.

It seemed as if all of Jerusalem had come out to see Jesus. That meant that all of Jerusalem also saw Duncan. The people shouted, "Hosanna! The King is here!"

"Wow!" Duncan thought. "I'm carrying a King!" And he held his head a little higher.

When Duncan arrived back home, his friends gathered around him eagerly.

"You did a great job!" said Carrie.

"Well done!" said Omar. Even Horace was impressed. "Wow, Duncan! You carried a King!"

Duncan no longer felt useless. He had played a part in a very special day for God's Son, Jesus.

"I wonder how God will use me next," thought Duncan. And he smiled.

For Parents

- Teach your children that God has a plan for them.
- Foster in them the patience to wait for God's perfect timing.
- Help them find ways to express their unique, God-given talents.

Children and adults alike often feel that they don't have a purpose. When we never have the chance to shine, we begin to wonder whether God created us with any sparkle at all. It becomes easy to see the successes of others while feeling that we are accomplishing little.

What does God have to say about us? "'For I know the plans I have for you,' declares the LORD, 'plans to prosper you and not to harm you, plans to give you hope and a future'" (Jeremiah 29:11 NIV). Duncan had been created by God to accomplish something very special. All he needed was the willingness to do God's work and the patience to watch His big plan unfold. When God finally revealed what he was to do, Duncan realized that God's purpose for him was bigger than he ever dreamed!

Tonight, take time to stop and pray with your children. Ask for God's guidance and vision. Ask for God to reveal to them His perfect plan for their lives. Below are some discussion questions that will help your children discover how God can use them.

Discussion Questions:

- Duncan wished he could be big like Horace, strong like Omar, or hard-working like Carrie. Do you ever wish you were better at certain things?
- What are some things that you are really good at? Ask your mom or dad what things they can do really well.
- Do you have older brothers and sisters or friends who can do things that you can't? Ask them to teach you new things or to let you help them with their jobs.
- Do you have younger brothers and sisters or friends who can't do everything that you can? Why not show them how to do new things or help them do little jobs that are just right for them.
- God had a special plan for Duncan. How can you find out God's special plans for you?